RICHARD SCARRY

Great Big
Air Book

RICHARD SCARRY

Great Big Air Book

First published in Great Britain in 1971
This edition published by HarperCollins Children's Books in 2007
HarperCollins Children's Books is a division of HarperCollins Publishers Ltd.

13 5 7 9 10 8 6 4 2
ISBN-13: 978-0-00-718944-1   ISBN-10: 0-00-718944-3

Printed and bound in China

HarperCollins *Children's Books*

A Spring Day

One spring morning a breeze blew a feather through the bedroom window.

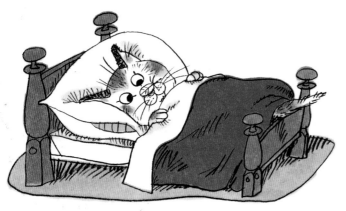

It tickled Huckle's nose.
"Aaah-chooo!" sneezed Huckle.

Huckle sneezed so hard that he blew Little Sister out of bed.
"Oh it must be windy today!" she said.

Huckle and Little Sister are breathing in
the fresh morning air.
Then they blow it out again.

You do it too. Breath in! Breathe out!
When you blow out, you make the air move.
You make a little wind of your own.

After breakfast, Miss Honey, the schoolteacher, stopped by to take the children for
a walk in the spring air. A strong wind came in the door with her.

It was a very windy day.
The children felt the wind pushing against them.
"Look at all the things the wind does," said Miss Honey.
"It makes the waves on the sea. It makes the clouds move and
the trees sway. It even dries the clothes on the clothesline."

The air becomes warmer in the springtime.
There is a sweet smell from the flowers and bugs fly back and
forth through the air. Flower seeds float on the spring breezes.
Colourful kites fly high in the sky.

Narcissus

Crocus

Lowly
Worm

Tulip

Daffodil

Violet

Lily o
the Va

Some people like to go for a drive
in the fresh spring air.

Dandelion

Farmer Fox ploughs his field for spring planting.
The plough loosens the soil so air and water can get in.
The roots of growing plants will need air and water.

"Oh, oh! It's going to rain," said Farmer Fox.
"My new tractor will get all wet."
Oops! I just felt a drop. I must hurry for shelter.

"Hurry, Mother Cat! Your laundry will get wet too. Hurry everyone! We must help Mummy bring the laundry into the house before it gets wet!"

Farmer Fox brought in Mummy's laundry just in time. He brought in his tractor too!
The laundry didn't get wet, and neither did his tractor.
Everyone gathered around to have tea and cocoa and cookies while waiting for the rain to stop.

In the kitchen Miss Honey had something else to show them.
"We all felt the big wind blowing outdoors today," she said.
"But right now, somewhere in this room, a little wind is blowing."
She borrowed Lowly Worm's tiny hat, and placed it over the spout of the
boiling teakettle.* Hot, steaming air was coming out of the spout.
Suddenly it began to lift Lowly's hat up off the spout.
"Hot air always rises," said Miss Honey. "The hot, steaming air
from the teakettle is making a little wind right here in the kitchen."

* Don't you ever do this yourself! You will get a burn!

"But don't worry, Lowly!
Your hat will come back down when the air cools off."

How Birds Fly

Birds can fly in the air.
Just watch Charlie Crow.
First, his legs push him into the air.

Then his wings open. They move upward and
forward as he pulls his legs close to his body.

GLUE

Then Charlie flaps his wings downward and to the rear.
His feathers close tightly together again. The downward
beat of his wings moves him forward in the air.
He uses his tail feathers to steer.
Now Charlie spreads his wings to slow down.
He is ready to land.

Oh, dear! He's stopped too fast!
He's a good flier, but he doesn't
always land so well.

Harry Hyena thinks that if he glues feathers on
his arms and tail – and then flaps his arms –
he will be able to fly like a bird.
Well, he is wrong.

Mother's Busy Day

Huck watched Mummy spray some perfume on herself. Air inside the little rubber ball forced a fine spray of perfume over her face and hair.

In the kitchen she turned on a fan to blow the smoke and cooking smells out of the house.

Then she used a vacuum cleaner to suck up dust and dirt from the floor.

Little Sister had nothing to do, so Mummy blew up her paddling pool. It took a lot of air.

Huckle wasn't bothering Mummy. He was kicking his ball. The ball was hard and firm because it was full of air.

Ha! Ha! You missed!

Some flies got into the house. Mummy chased them with a can of insect spray. Air in the can forced out the spray.

Then Mummy washed some clothes. Hot air in the clothes drier dried the clean laundry.

She baked a pie and left it on the window sill for the breeze to cool.

While she was driving to town, Mummy noticed that one tyre was soft. She blew it up again with an air pump. Not too much air now, Mamma!

At the hairdresser she sat under the hairdryer. The warm air dried her freshly washed hair.

Back home again, Mummy started supper. But when she tried to light the oven, a strong breeze blew out the match. Then another. And another!

After a while she said "I just wish that breeze would stop blowing."
"But, Mummy," said Huckle, "if air didn't move and blow around, you couldn't have done all the things you did today."
"I guess you are right," she said.
And with her very next match she was able to light the oven.

A Summer Picnic

It was a bright, sunny summer day. There was not a cloud in the sky.
Miss Honey and her boyfriend, Bruno, decided to take all the children on a picnic.

They drove past a lake where
some fishermen were fishing.
Oh, oh! They seem to have caught something!

While they were setting out the picnic, Rudolf Strudel,
the famous airplane pilot, dropped by.
"Miss Honey!" he said. "A big thunderstorm is coming this way!
You and the children must take shelter immediately!"

Ants always
come to picnics!

Everyone had been too busy putting out food to
notice the black storm clouds gathering in the sky.
"Hurry!" Rudolf warned. "The rain will start any minute."

C-r-a-a-a-a-a-c-c-k-k-k!
The lightening flashed! The thunder roared!
But everyone was safely inside the school bus.

No one got even the tiniest bit wet.
Not even Farmer Fox's tractor.
It was the best rainy-day picnic ever.

How Aeroplanes Fly

control tower

Father Cat took Huckle and Little Sister to the airport to meet Rudolf, the famous pilot. He was going to show them how to fly an airplane.

First, Rudolf pointed to the cockpit. "The pilot sits here," he said. "He flies the airplane with the stick, the throttle and the pedals. The stick is used to move the elevators on the rear wings up and down. They help the plane to fly lower or higher.

"The stick also moves with ailerons on the front wings up and down. These help to make the plane tip sideways and turn. The pedals move the rudder on the tail. This helps the plane to turn smoothly."

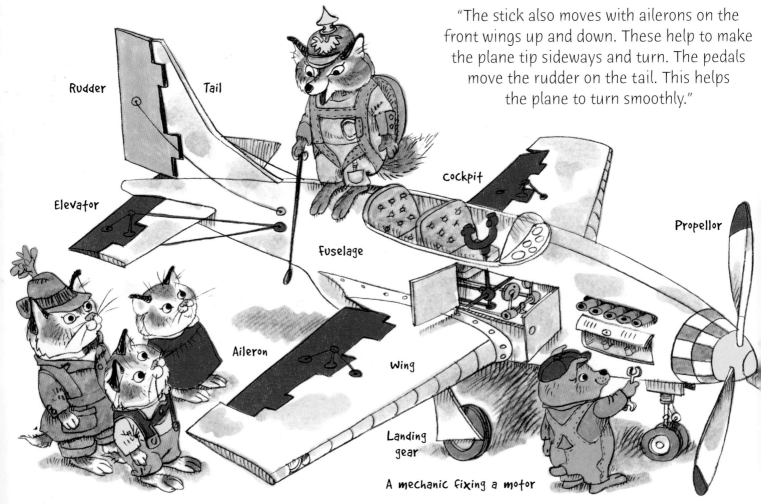

Rudder

Tail

Elevator

Cockpit

Propellor

Fuselage

Aileron

Wing

Landing gear

A mechanic fixing a motor

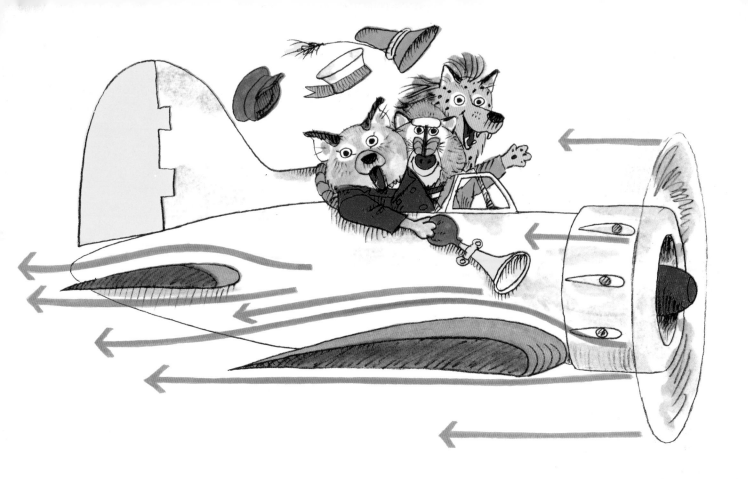

"The spinning propeller pulls the plane forward, and makes the air slip around the wing.
The air that goes over the curved top of the wing moves fast. But along
the straight bottom of the wing the air moves slower.
This makes it push harder, and it lifts the plane up, up into the sky."

"One day I'll fly an airplane," said Huckle.
"Yes, maybe," said Rudolf. "But for now
come flying with me."

Huck Takes Flying Lessons

"First, everyone fasten his seatbelt," said Rudolf.
"I will start the engine and set the propeller to spinning.
Down the runway we speed. Faster! Faster!"

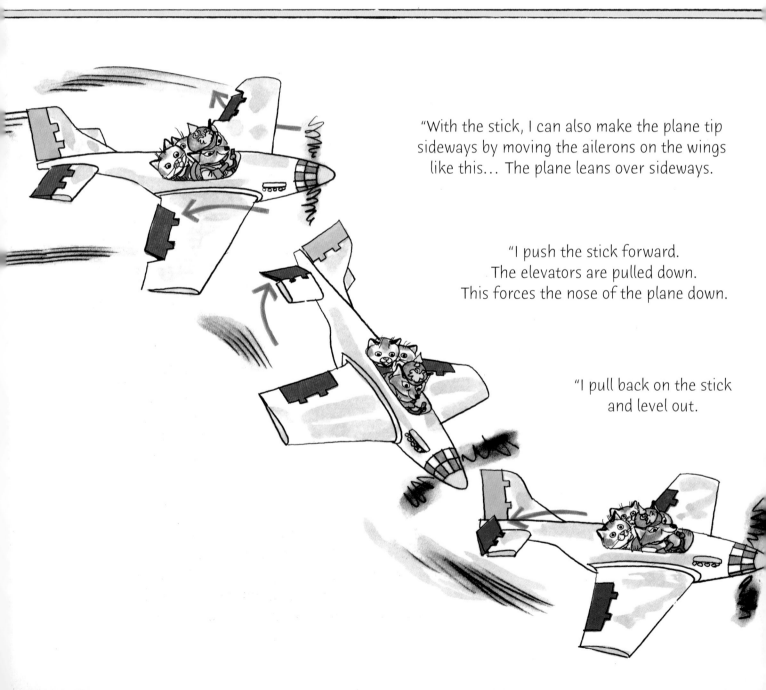

"With the stick, I can also make the plane tip
sideways by moving the ailerons on the wings
like this… The plane leans over sideways.

"I push the stick forward.
The elevators are pulled down.
This forces the nose of the plane down.

"I pull back on the stick
and level out.

"I'll pull back on the stick. The elevators are pulled up.
The moving air strikes them and pushes the tail down. This, together with the
pressure under the wings, forces the nose up. I fold up the landing gear and push
the stick forward a little bit. Now we are flying level."

"Then I turn over. I...!

"Now I climb steeply.

"Oh! Oh! I've fallen out!
I forgot to fasten my seat belt!

"But I, Rudolf Strudel, am lucky!
I never fail to wear my parachute.
The air is trapped in the parachute letting me
fall slowly to earth. But I wonder if Huckle will
be able to land the plane safely all by himself?"

Huck Lands the Plane

Huckle quickly grabbed the control stick and located the pedals.

By working the rudder, the ailerons, and the elevators just as Rudolf had shown him, he started to come down and land.

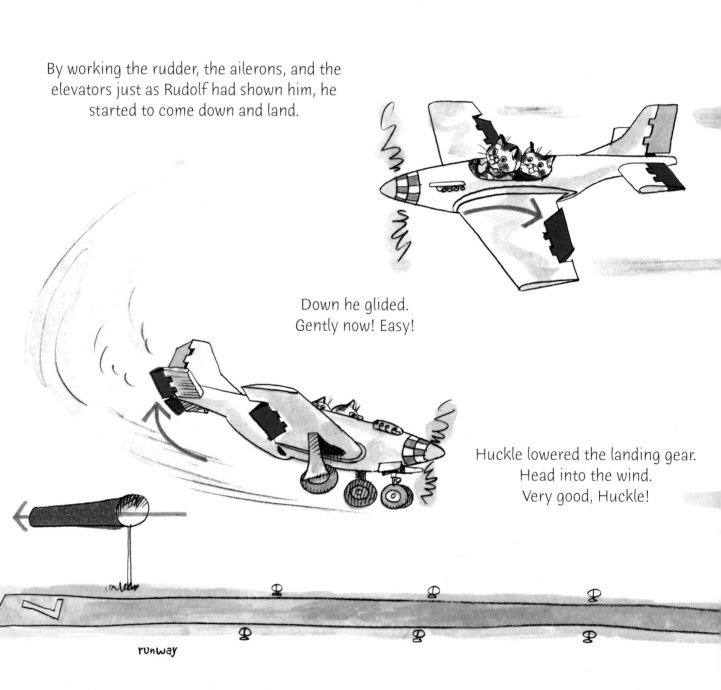

Down he glided.
Gently now! Easy!

Huckle lowered the landing gear.
Head into the wind.
Very good, Huckle!

runway

Touchdown! A perfect landing.
You are an excellent pilot, Huckle.

...And another perfect landing.
Right in the pickle barrel!
Very good, Rudolf.

There is a fair at the airport.
Everyone has come to see, or take rides in, the old
fashioned airplanes. All these old airplanes have
propellers to help them fly through the air.

Attention, all pilots!
Please do not bump into any runaway balloons.

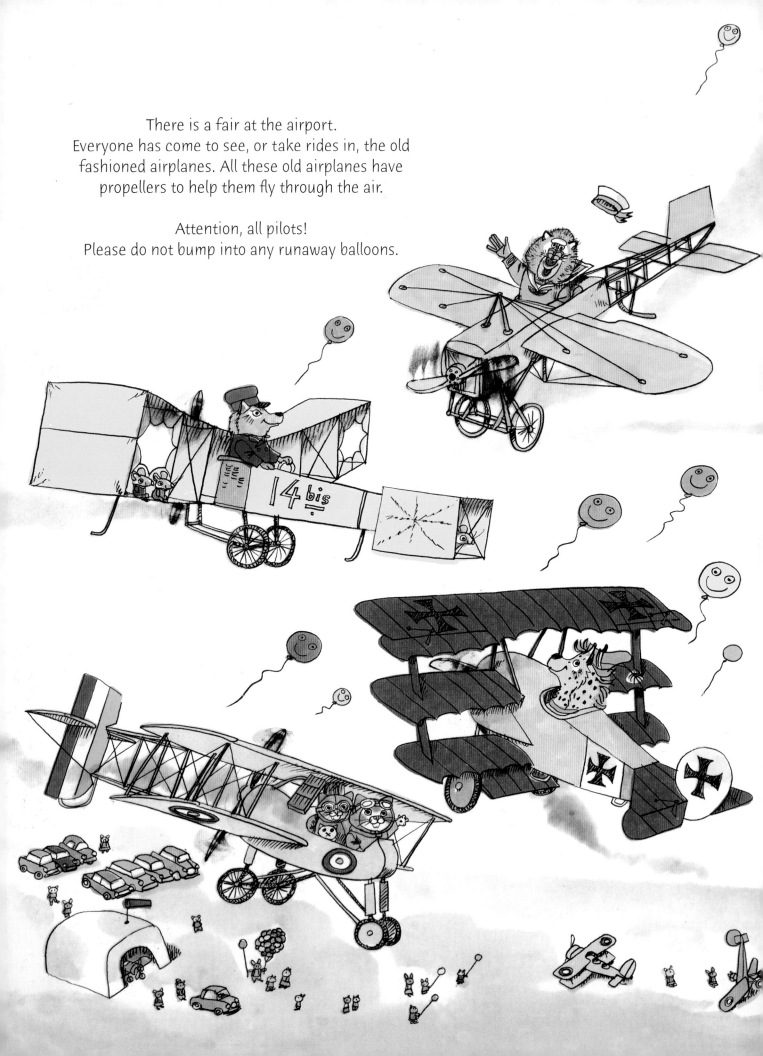

There is a new jet airplane at the fair, too.
Jet planes don't need propellers to make them fly.

Look at Benny Baboon. He is going to show you
something with a toy balloon.

First, he blows up the balloon with air.
But he does not tie a knot in it.
Instead, he lets go of the balloon.
The air begins to rush out of the hole at
the end. As the air rushes out, it pushes
the balloon away from Benny.

control tower

weatherman

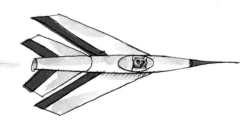

The air is going…

going…

gone!

Rudolf's jet plane engine works a little like a balloon.
Up front, air is sucked into the engine.

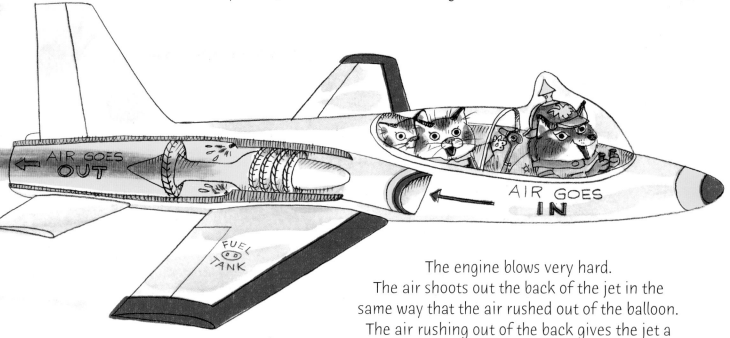

← AIR GOES OUT

AIR GOES IN

FUEL TANK

The engine blows very hard.
The air shoots out the back of the jet in the
same way that the air rushed out of the balloon.
The air rushing out of the back gives the jet a
powerful push forward.

V-r-r-o-o-o-o-m-m-m-m!

The Cat family was going to visit Grandma on her birthday,
They rode in a taxi to the small country airport nearby.

There they climbed into a helicopter
to go to the big city airport.

On the way, they saw Sergeant Murphy down below.
He was unscrambling a big traffic jam. Everyone seemed
to be heading towards the airport.

At the city airport, the whirling blades gently lowered the helicopter to the ground.
For the rest of the journey the Cat family would be travelling by jet airliner.

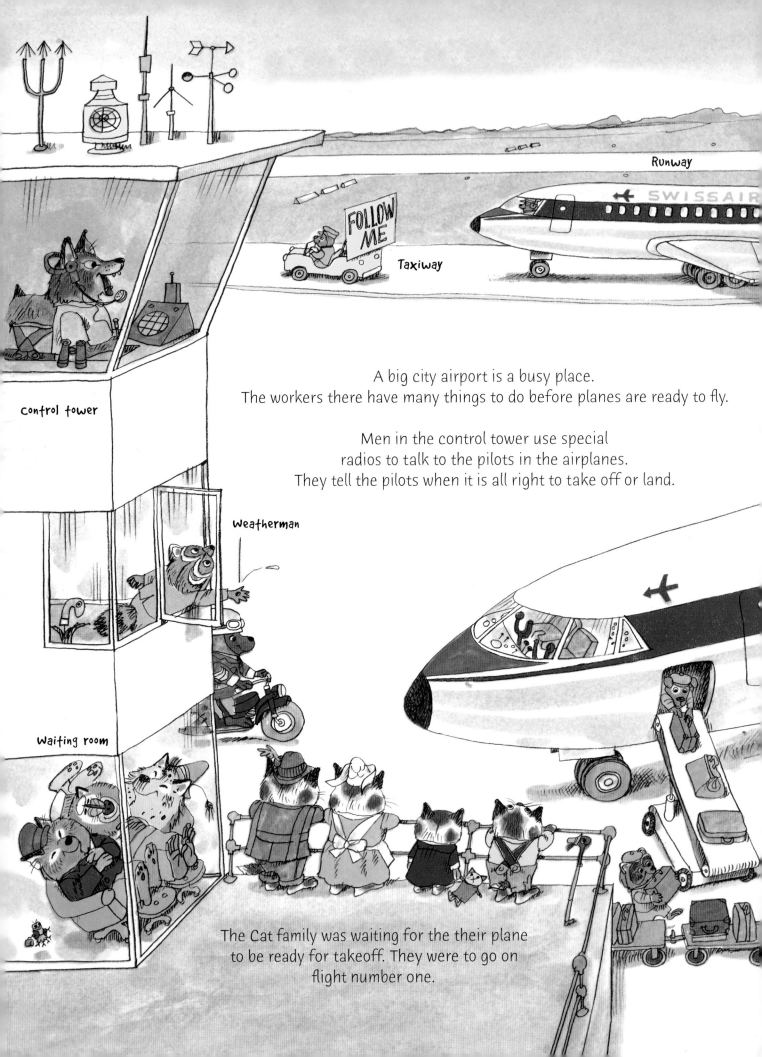

Runway

FOLLOW ME

Taxiway

SWISSAIR

control tower

Weatherman

Waiting room

A big city airport is a busy place.
The workers there have many things to do before planes are ready to fly.

Men in the control tower use special
radios to talk to the pilots in the airplanes.
They tell the pilots when it is all right to take off or land.

The Cat family was waiting for the their plane
to be ready for takeoff. They were to go on
flight number one.

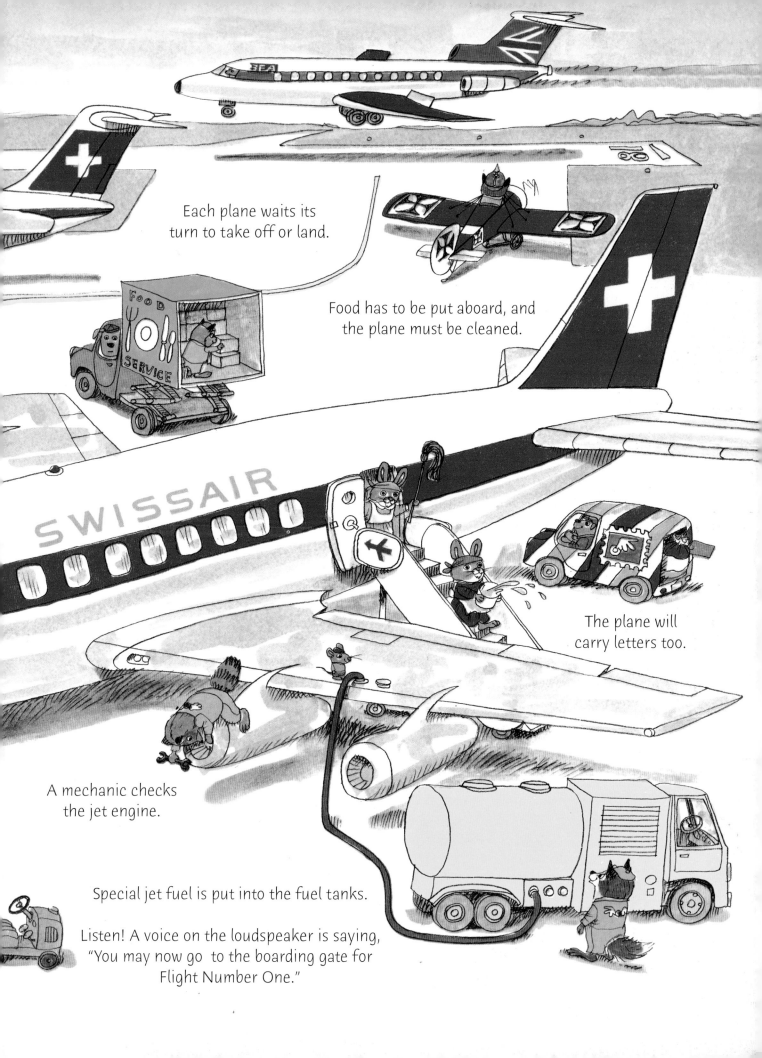

Each plane waits its turn to take off or land.

Food has to be put aboard, and the plane must be cleaned.

The plane will carry letters too.

A mechanic checks the jet engine.

Special jet fuel is put into the fuel tanks.

Listen! A voice on the loudspeaker is saying, "You may now go to the boarding gate for Flight Number One."

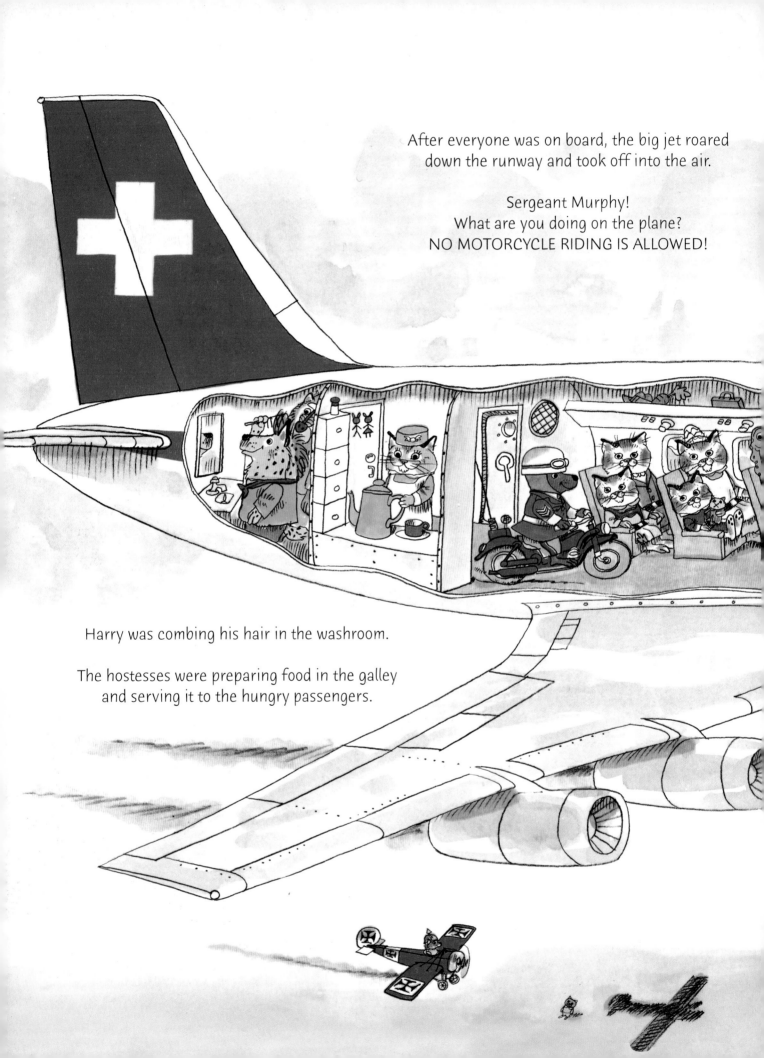

After everyone was on board, the big jet roared down the runway and took off into the air.

Sergeant Murphy!
What are you doing on the plane?
NO MOTORCYCLE RIDING IS ALLOWED!

Harry was combing his hair in the washroom.

The hostesses were preparing food in the galley and serving it to the hungry passengers.

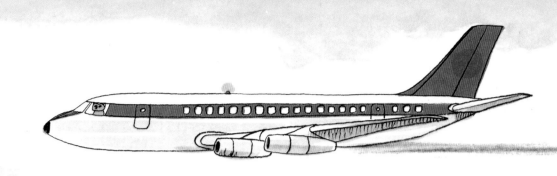

Every plane flies in the air lane assigned to it.
In that way, planes don't bump into each other.

Captain Fox is flying the plane with the help of his co-pilot.
The navigator is planning the plane's route in the sky.

NAVIGATOR

"Attention, please!
This is your captain speaking.
Everybody fasten his seatbelt.
We are about to land."

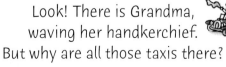

Look! There is Grandma,
waving her handkerchief.
But why are all those taxis there?

The Cat family's plane landed, and Lowly gave Grandma a big kiss.
A lot of other planes landed, too.
Everyone was coming to Grandma's birthday party.
That was why Grandma brought along so many taxis.
They were going to take all her friends to her house.

Sergeant Murphy had come along just to unscramble the big taxi jam!
A good thing, too, or no one would ever get to the party.

"Why, Rudolf!" shouted Sergeant Murphy.
"How did you ever get your plane into this taxi jam?"

Air is very important for blowing
out birthday candles.
Grandma's cake had so many candles
she couldn't blow them out all by herself,
So all her friends helped her.
W-H-O-O-O-O-S-H!
Happy Birthday, Grandma!

Grandma had such a good time at her party that she can hardly wait until next year.

In the autumn the leaves fall from the trees.
The smell of burning leaves is in the air.
Farmer Fox and his family and friends must
gather the crops before the cold winter comes.

Philip is carrying grain to the mill.
The wind makes the windmill spin.
Inside the mill, the grain is ground into flour.
Bread will be made with the flour.

armer Fox is picking
juicy red apples.

OLD FARMER FOX'S
ROADSIDE STAND

Nuts

Toffee
apples

Jelly

Apples

Apple cider

Mother Fox sells the harvest foods at her roadside stand.
Just a minute! Look there!
Do you see what Huckle sees,?

A FIRE!!!
It has reached Farmer Fox's ladder!
Hurry, Mrs Fox! Call the firemen.

Before Mother Fox can hang up the phone, the firemen come racing to the rescue.

Smokey, the fireman, turns on the water too soon. The hose wiggles and squirms out of control, squirting water everywhere!

OLD FARMER FOX'S
ROADSIDE STAND

APPLES

WATER 17

WATER 17

The force of the water is knocking apples and apple pickers out of the trees. Someone, please grab that hose!

Huckle finally gets hold of it and puts out the fire. He has saved Farmer Fox's roadside stand from burning down. Water can put out fires because it keeps air away from them. Fires can't burn without air.

Farmer Fox gives everyone a toffee apple to celebrate. Mmmm! Toffee apples taste delicious in the crisp autumn air.

When Huckle beats his drum, the top of it shakes back and forth very fast. This makes a loud noise. The sound speeds through the air. Mother Cat hears it with her ears.

The door opens and in walks Miss Honey with the class orchestra. They are going to practise at Huckle's house today. What has Miss Honey got in that huge case?

At last everyone has an instrument unpacked and ready to play. "Get set! Play!" says Miss Honey, and the music begins.

Bass drum

Violin

cymbals

Miss Honey plays the fiddle

Piano

Accordion

Guitar

Harp

Bassoon

Trumpet

Saxophone

Tuba

clarinet

Some instruments are played by blowing into them.
The air inside moves back and forth very fast.
This makes the sound your ears hear.

Flute

Trombone

But Huckle beats his drum with drumsticks,
while Lowly sings very loudly.
"Ow-wa-e-e-a-a-h-h-a-," goes Lowly's voice.

The sounds that Huckle and his friends
make travel through the air. Their music is
so loud that it shakes Mother Cat and Little
Sister right out of their chairs!

Huckle and the class orchestra certainly know
how to make themselves heard, don't they?

In the wintertime the air is very cold.
Instead of rain, there is often snow. The strong winds howl and blow.
Sometimes the snow falls and falls, getting deeper and deeper.
This kind of snow is called a blizzard.
Blizzards can cause a lot of trouble.

The firemen were trying to get to Ma Pig's to put out a fire in her kitchen.
But a snowplough had to plough a path for them.
Would they get there in time?

Railway crossing

Pa Pig was riding home from work in the train.
But tonight it was stuck in a snow drift.
Would he have to spend the night there?

The wind and snow and ice had knocked down the electric wires. Many houses and no light. Others had no heat.

The delivery man and the school bus were both stuck in the snow.

Doctor Dog was tramping through the snow on snowshoes. He was trying to visit a sick patient. "Will this snow never stop falling?" he asked.

At last the snow did stop falling.
The blizzard ended. Pa Pig finally got home from work.
The firemen put out the fire in time.
Doctor Dog saw his sick patient.
But the school bus and the deliveryman were still stuck in the drifts.
"No school today!" said Miss Honey.
Instead, everyone had fun playing out in the snow.

Saucer

Sledge

Be careful Miss Honey!

Skis

Ski

Snowball

Snow fort

Just look at all the things you can do
in the clear, cold, winter air.

Chalet

Snowshoes

Snowcat

Snowman

You can even make a tiny cloud with your breath.

Hockey stick

Ice skater

Ice rink

A trip to the Moon

Wolfgang Wolf, Benny Baboon, and Harry Hyena
are about to climb aboard their spacecraft.
They are going to the moon to collect rock
samples and bring them back to the Earth.
They want to find out what the moon is made of.

Ready for lift-off.
Five, four, three, two, one, LIFT-OFF!
Up, up goes the spaceship – off into
space and heading for the moon.

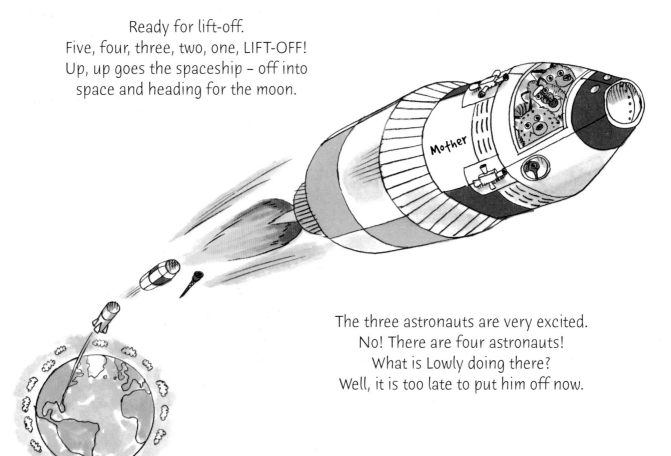

The three astronauts are very excited.
No! There are four astronauts!
What is Lowly doing there?
Well, it is too late to put him off now.

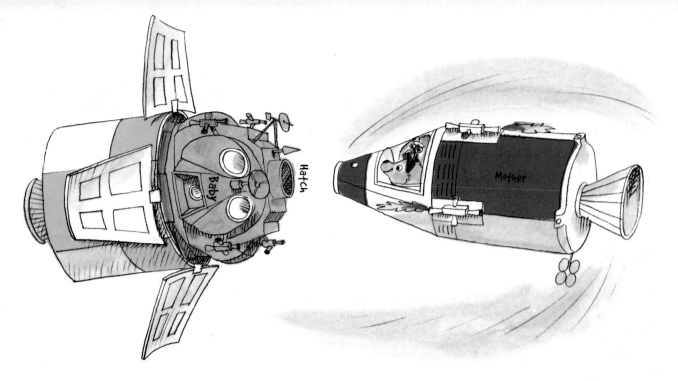

The spacecraft is getting close to the moon.
The landing ship (Baby) is attached to the command ship (Mother).
Wolfgang turns the nose of the command ship around so it fits into
the hatch door of the landing ship.

Then Benny, Harry and Lowly climb through
the hatch door into the landing ship.
Wolfgang stays behind in the command ship
to wait for their return.
The two ships separate so that the landing
ship can head for the moon.

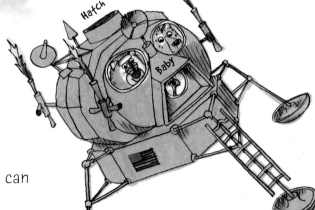

Benny! Turn on your landing motor so you can
make a gentle landing on the moon.

The ship trips over a rock.
It does not land very gently.

There is no air on the moon.
Each astronaut has to carry his air
with him. It is carried in a tank in the
pack on the astronaut's back.
But Lowly has no space suit so
he gets into Harry's suit.
Now he can breathe air.
Pick, pick, pick.
They are busy collecting rock samples.

It is time to climb back into the landing ship.
The air in the astronauts' tanks is almost all used up.
Inside the landing ship there is plenty of air for breathing.

Oh, dear!
The hatch door won't
stay closed!

The air inside the landing ship will leak out.
"Keep calm," says Lowly. "Benny, you hold the door shut. Harry, you turn
on the air tank. Then I will be able to breathe when I get out of your spacesuit.
I know how to keep the hatch door closed."

Lowly ties himself into a knot around the door
handle, and the door stays tightly shut.
"Now we will be able to get back with our
valuable rocks," says Lowly.

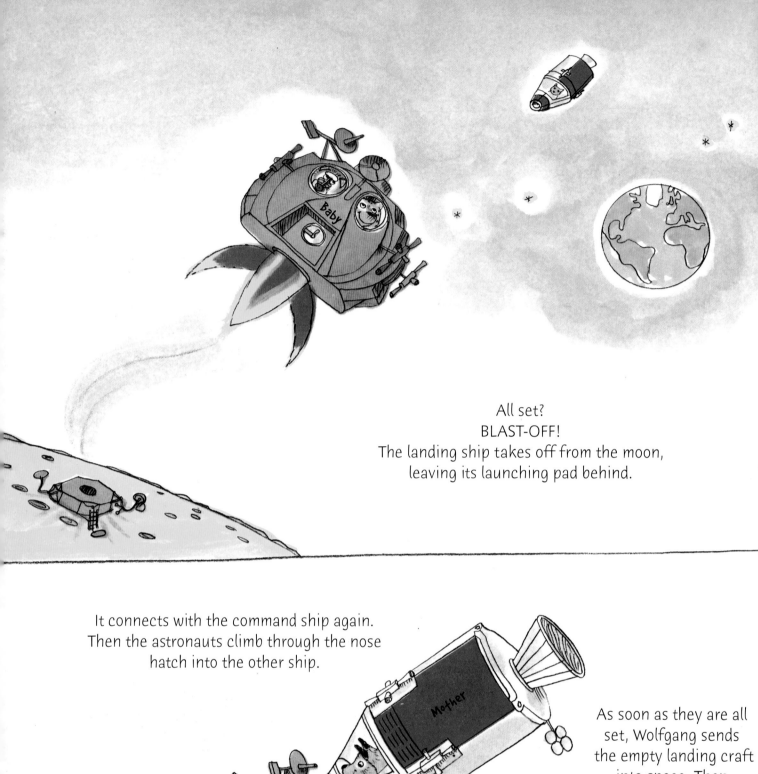

All set?
BLAST-OFF!
The landing ship takes off from the moon,
leaving its launching pad behind.

It connects with the command ship again.
Then the astronauts climb through the nose
hatch into the other ship.

As soon as they are all
set, Wolfgang sends
the empty landing craft
into space. Then
the command ship
heads back to earth.

After the astronauts get back into the earth's atmosphere,
they open up the big parachutes on their spaceship.
An aircraft carrier and several helicopters are waiting to pick them up out of the sea.
HERE THEY COME...

But the spaceship does not land in the water.
It goes… RIGHT DOWN THE FUNNEL!
Well anyway, the astronauts have landed safely
with their precious rocks.

Everyone is happy to see the brave astronauts safely back on earth.

After they have all had a bath, the admiral gives Lowly a shiny medal.
On the medal are the words:

"Lowly Worm, a real astro-knot.
The first worm on the moon."

Lowly likes his medal very much,
But best of all he likes being back on earth
where he can breathe fresh air again!
All right, everyone! Let's all take a deep breath
of the earth's wonderful air!